PSYCHIC SCIENCE

PSYCHIC
SCIENCE

SINKHOLE

PSYCHIC SCIENCE

KELLI HICKS

DARBY CREEK

MINNEAPOLIS

Darby Creek
An imprint of Lerner Publishing Group, Inc.
241 First Avenue North
Minneapolis, MN 55401 USA

For reading levels and more information, look up this title at www.lernerbooks.com.

Cover and interior images: Copyright ©2019 Aleksandar Grozdanovski/Shutterstock (background); solar22/Shutterstock (zombie); Milano M (chapter number background)

Main body text set in Janson Text LT Std.
Typeface provided by Adobe Systems.

Library of Congress Cataloging-in-Publication Data

Names: Hicks, Kelli L., author.
Title: Psychic science / Kelli Hicks.
Description: Minneapolis : Darby Creek, [2023] | Series: Sinkhole | Audience: Ages 11–18. | Audience: Grades 10–12. | Summary: In spite of their differing opinions—while Anna believes in science, Caleb pursues the paranormal for his social media program—the two friends must work together when a strange purple mist turns the animals and people of Foggy Creek, Texas, into zombie-like creatures.
Identifiers: LCCN 2022023505 (print) | LCCN 2022023506 (ebook) | ISBN 9781728475516 (library binding) | ISBN 9781728477985 (paperback) | ISBN 9781728479552 (ebook)
Subjects: CYAC: Supernatural—Fiction. | LCGFT: Paranormal fiction. | High interest-low vocabulary books. | Novels.
Classification: LCC PZ7.1.H5437 Ps 2023 (print) | LCC PZ7.1.H5437 (ebook) | DDC [Fic]—dc23

LC record available at https://lccn.loc.gov/2022023505
LC ebook record available at https://lccn.loc.gov/2022023506

Manufactured in the United States of America
1 – TR – 12/15/22

Caleb and Anna walked toward their last period classrooms. He had computer science. Hers was calculus. The classrooms were right next door to each other.

Today, he pulled out a photo of a mysterious creature. "Check this out," he said. "This sighting is legit."

"You could not be more wrong, Caleb. Don't you get tired of having this same argument over and over again? These creatures are not real."

"I could not be more right about this, Anna. Don't you get tired of being so boring?" he asked.

Anna let out a frustrated breath. She pushed her shoulders back and closed her eyes. "Listen, Caleb. There is no proof that there is a strange, hairy beast roaming the city."

It was Caleb's turn to pause and think before saying something that was going to make him sound ridiculous. Or worse, make Anna think she was right.

"Anna, there is a witness. He has a picture. It is a credible sighting."

"I know you believe in this paranormal stuff, Caleb. But the witness is an older man with poor vision, and he has made these unfounded claims before. The picture shows a blurry image. This is not proof. It could be a total fake. I am walking away now, Caleb. This conversation is over."

After Anna stormed out of the computer lab's doorway, Caleb looked at the photo and sighed. Then he made his way to his computer desk. He sat down and waited for Ms. Smith's instructions. It wasn't long before he was lost in a daydream.

He and Anna had been friends since they were in kindergarten. When they were little, Anna always got excited about going on an adventure and usually agreed to go along with Caleb's ideas and schemes. He never suggested anything that could have gotten them hurt or was overly dangerous, but they used to have fun.

He remembered one time when they were about eight or nine years old, they rode their bikes all the way to the sinkholes at the edge of town. If their parents knew, they would have been grounded forever. They found a small puddle and decided it looked fun. It was strange to have standing water anywhere during the dry Texas weather in Foggy Creek, but the air was scorching so they splashed like a couple of wild birds taking a bath. The puddle was much deeper than they thought it was going to be. Soon, they were taking turns digging down into the water and grabbing whatever their hands touched. He remembered the feel of thick, black mud oozing through his fingers and what seemed like sticks that poked his hands as he blindly grabbed under the water. He even thought he felt something squirmy brush against his fingers. He jerked his hand out of the water as fast as he could. Anna's laughter, though, kept him hanging around the puddle of water longer than he wanted to be there. Anna was fearless. She kept digging deeper and deeper until, suddenly, she got really wide-eyed and let loose a high-pitched squeal.

"Holy cow, Caleb. Look at this! Have you ever seen anything like this before?"

Her hands came out of the puddle holding a weird fishlike thing. He thought it might be what brushed against his fingers when he dug into the mud. The thing wiggled in her hands. It shimmered in the sunlight, a silvery greenish creature with four small, webbed feet and a long, scaled tail that whipped back and forth. Two small cone shapes stuck out from the side of its face. And it had only one eye! It was so creepy.

Anna shouted. "Caleb! Help!"

The creature dug deep into her skin. Blood poured from the puncture wounds on her hand. Caleb grabbed Anna's hand and hit the creature against the ground until it let go and disappeared down into the water by the sinkhole. He had never seen anything so strange before.

Even though Caleb knew Anna always tried to be brave, he could tell that her hand was aching. Her lip quivered slightly. Tears welled up in her big brown eyes. Caleb was angry at himself for not recognizing the danger, for not paying closer attention. He was mad he didn't make Anna leave earlier. Then she wouldn't have gotten bit. Caleb took a bandana out of his pocket and wrapped it around Anna's hand.

"Hold on, Anna. I know your hand hurts, but I'll take care of you. Can you make it back to my house?"

Anna sniffled and nodded her head.

"Climb on the back of my bike," he told her.

She did and he pedaled them back to town, Anna's arms around his waist, clinging to him as they bounced across the rocky terrain. His legs had ached from the long, tough ride, but he knew he had to get that wound cleaned so it wouldn't get infected.

Because his house was closer, he took Anna there. Then he poured peroxide on her wound. Her quick intake of breath told him that the peroxide stung, but she continued to hold still. He bandaged her hand carefully with some gauze and medical tape. They never told anyone about what happened because they both knew how upset their parents would have been if they found out they had been so far away, exploring the sinkholes. Instead, they told her parents she scraped her hand on the playground.

This adventure always stuck with him because they never did find out what that creature was. Nor did they ever see anything like it again. For Caleb, it was the start of his fascination with weird creatures and otherworldly happenings. For Anna, it seemed the strange event sparked her interest in science and finding answers to prove why or how something worked.

As they continued through school, Anna's

interests seemed to grow further and further apart from Caleb's. She became more and more interested in science and facts. She thrived on pressure and loved to have deadlines. In an almost constant search for "the truth," she searched for data to support her ideas and worked hard to do her best in school. By the time they got to high school, he saw her change from a fun-loving friend to a driven, focused high-achiever. She was organized and always prepared. But, it seemed to Caleb, she didn't know how to have fun anymore. He found it sad. The only thing that she did for fun was play on the golf team, although that didn't seem all that fun to him. She wasn't that good at the game, but she said it would look good on a college application. Anna was clearly taking the recommendation from her guidance counselor who said a "well-rounded" student stood out on college applications.

Ms. Smith's voice startled Caleb out of his memories of Anna and their childhood. Remembering he had homework to turn in, he logged on and uploaded his project. Soon enough, he glanced at the clock and realized it was three o'clock. The last bell would ring in fifteen minutes.

He waited all day for that bell because it signaled that it was finally time to work on things he really wanted to: creating content for his ViewTube Channel. Thankfully, Ms. Smith let Caleb hang around the lab after school and use as much of the equipment as he needed. Aside from computer science class, Caleb found the routines and structure of school, and Anna, for that matter, to be terribly frustrating. He didn't have the time or the patience for the kind of research and data collecting that Anna enjoyed. He saw himself as more open-minded than Anna. He liked drama and excitement and loved hearing stories about all the weird and wonderful things that happened in and around his town. He wanted others to know about these cool and seemingly unbelievable things, too. That's why he started his own ViewTube channel. The channel gave him a way to connect with people. He was good with words and knew how to get people riled up and interested in new ideas and bizarre events.

Opening up his notebook, Caleb leaned over and began writing the script for his upcoming video. Caleb knew that sometimes he stretched the truth to tell a good story, but he needed to keep people interested so that they would continue to tune in. The more followers he had, the more solid his future was going to be. Caleb knew he wasn't college material. He needed to find a different path. One that was exciting and made enough money to give him the chance to travel and investigate the paranormal on a larger scale. Caleb shook his head. Enough worrying about Anna and the past. It was time to find a new story.

2

When the last bell of the day rang, Anna
hurried down the hallway. She needed to stop
letting Caleb get to her. He lived in a dream
world, and she needed to be serious. After
stopping at her locker, she looked through her
planner, deciding which textbooks to leave at
school and which to take home. Just calculus
and English homework tonight, but it wouldn't
hurt to brush up on world history for the
upcoming test. She put the three huge books
in her backpack. Then she looked at her watch
and realized she was late. And she hated to

be late. As the president of the science club, the meeting couldn't start until she arrived. The club was studying chemical compounds and how the substitution of one bond could dramatically change the compound.

"Sorry I'm late. I ran into Caleb before last period," Anna said. "He's got me all upset about the latest mystery creature sighting in Foggy Creek." She shook her head in frustration.

"Oh, Caleb, eh? Did you see his last upload? It was awesome. Did you know he actually saw a ghost?"

"I don't pay any attention when he talks nonsense," Anna replied. "He has an active imagination. And I can't believe that you, Jesse, a true believer in science, would actually think his story is true."

"Well, anybody that cute can't be that bad. Right?" Jesse let out a little giggle and Anna shook her head.

"Can we forget about Caleb and start our meeting?" Anna said. "We have several compounds to test. And did everyone bring their envelopes? We'll open them together. After we finish the experiments."

The members of the club had been holding on to the admission letters they received from various colleges. Anna had made them agree to open the letters together so they could support each other. No matter what was in the letters. Together, they could celebrate their success or help each other with disappointment.

But, first, experiments. The club got down to business. They put on safety goggles and gloves. They brought out the necessary solutions and carefully conducted their experiments. Anna let her mind wander while they were working. She remembered the old times with Caleb. He used to think he was so fearless. But she was actually the adventurous one. When the strange sinkholes first opened up, she was the one who wanted to check them out. Caleb thought the idea was too scary. Eventually, they went to check them out together and she let Caleb believe it was his idea. They used to ride their bikes everywhere.

Anna smiled, remembering the freedom of being younger. Her parents worked all the time to provide for their family, and she spent a lot of time on her own. It didn't really bother her because she had Caleb to keep her company. She never did anything outrageous, but she loved biking around town and hanging out with Caleb. Now, things were different. She had to be focused. She had to get into the best college, and she needed a scholarship. Her parents were first-generation Americans. They worked hard to buy a small, cozy house in town and to care for Anna. Anna couldn't afford to goof off. She had to stay on track to be able to make her parents proud. One day, she hoped to be able to help take care of them. Anna snapped back to reality and back to testing compounds.

Working diligently, Anna created chemical compounds and tested out the stability of each. She counted on completing their research and presenting it at the state science competition, knowing it could earn them all college scholarships. Her big college dreams required money. And she needed a financial miracle to make those dreams come true.

"Hey, Anna! I'm dying to open these college letters. Are you ready?" Stephanie asked.

"Yes! Let's do it," she replied. "But we need to clean up first."

They cleaned up from their experiments and put their materials away. They hung up their lab coats and washed their hands.

Stephanie went first. Her hands shook as she tried to open the envelope in her hand.

"Anna, you're going to have to do it for me," she said. "I'm too nervous. I don't know what I'll do if I don't get in."

Anna took the envelope and tore the end off. She took out the letter from State University, Stephanie's dream school. Anna's eyes darted back and forth as she read the words: *You are receiving this letter to inform you of your application status to our prestigious State University. Due to your high test scores, strong community service, and outstanding essay, we are pleased to offer you acceptance into the chemistry program. Congratulations!*

"You did it! You got in!" Anna said, truly happy for her friend.

Everyone cheered.

More envelopes opened with many rounds of applause and cheering.

Finally, it was Anna's turn. She was the only science club member who had applied to Tech, which was known for its biochemistry program. As a small college, it was harder to get into. She took a deep breath and began reading:

Thank you for your admissions application. As you know, our program is highly competitive. Before we offer any seats, we need to interview you in person. Dr. Susan Ebright, the head of our biochemistry department, will be coming to meet with you on your high school campus.

Anna felt let down. She also felt very nervous.

"It's great you got the interview," Stephanie said. "I know once that professor meets you that she will want to offer you a spot. You've got this."

"I hope you're right," Anna replied. It was hard to express how much she wanted to get into this program.

Anna's heart pounded in her chest. Impressing the head of the department would be no easy feat. Anna knew she would have to really wow Dr. Ebright. It was the only way to get into her dream school and get the financial aid that she needed. She read the rest of the letter, paying close attention to the stated interview date and time. Then she added the interview date to the calendar app on her phone. *One more hurdle*, she thought. *Time to practice my responses for Dr. Ebright's interview.*

On the other side of campus, Caleb settled into
the computer lab's studio where he recorded
the videos for his channel. He had permission
to use the broadcast booth that belonged to
the school news team. They had an amazing
setup with state-of-the-art webcams, noise-
reducing headphones, and a great collection
of music and sound effects that he could use
in his broadcasts. His social media following
seemed to increase daily. He reported on all
the strange happenings and paranormal events
in the town. The more bizarre the story, the

more followers he gained. Everyone in town knew that Caleb was the one to go to when they had a tale to tell. Floating orbs, doors that opened on their own, and furniture moving without anyone touching it. All these strange things seemed to happen in Foggy Creek on a regular basis.

People felt comfortable sharing their experiences with Caleb. They knew he was open-minded and curious. Unfortunately, sometimes he questioned if the video was real or staged. But he still shared them as if they were one hundred percent true. In his mind, he was just giving the people what they wanted. Mystery. Entertainment. Excitement.

He put on his headphones, checked the settings, and prepped the lighting. He glanced at his script and was soon ready to tell his stories to the camera.

"Hey there, friends, fellow students, and followers of the bizarre. It's me, Caleb Henderson, and have I got a story for you. Last night, local resident Mr. George Jacobs was letting his dog outside. You know, to take care of business. He saw movement to his left, but thought it was just a raccoon or maybe a rat headed for the garbage cans. He has had trouble with that. Anyway, he goes over, thinking he needs to chase these pests away when he hears a strange growl. Not a sound you would hear from a raccoon. Mr. Jacobs gets closer and yells out, 'hey . . . get out of my trash!' You can imagine his surprise when the creature turns and two glowing yellow eyes stare him down. Bigger than a raccoon but smaller than a bear, this thing's body was covered in shaggy fur. He said its stench smelled like the toilet overflowed and got covered in skunk spray. Gross! Mr. Jacobs is lucky he didn't hurt himself as he runs back to the house to get a shovel, or a tennis racket, or something to take a swing at this thing. At the house, he remembers to grab his phone. As he approaches the cans, it seems pretty quiet. He thinks maybe the creature is gone. Then . . . SCREECH, he hears this horrible scream, drops his shovel, and runs like a track star for the safety of his house. He climbs the front steps and swings open the front door. Right before the door slams, he turns and snaps this picture of the monster. Go online and take a look at this thing. Creepy!"

Pausing to catch his breath, Caleb added a spooky sound effect to entertain his audience.

Then he went on sharing his accounts where the picture would be posted. Caleb reminded his viewers to contact him if they'd had a similar experience before wrapping up this episode with his usual call for stories. "Any strange beasts or apparitions roaming your house? Give me a call! Well, thanks for watching. I'll be back soon with another story of the unusual. Stay safe, my friends. I'm out!"

Caleb shut down the camera and uploaded the video. Then he figured he'd check back later to see what his viewers thought. This was a solid story, but he needed a bigger story than this. He was going to have to really dig deep and find something new and special to share with his audience.

Later that evening, Caleb racked his brain

to try to think of an idea for another great story. He did a special on bigfoot sightings. He shared reports of ghosts and even a few alien encounters. Because of the strange sinkholes, people tuned in to his channel to see the wild things reported in Foggy Creek. But he felt like he needed a different kind of story. Something new, something really unusual, something to increase his number of followers and get more sponsors, all of which would mean money. He might even be an international paranormal celebrity someday.

Caleb texted Anna.

> Caleb: Did you see my upload? You were wrong about the picture. Everybody believes it. I think the yellow eyes really drew them in.

Caleb saw the dots moving. Laughing quietly, he just knew Anna was going to tell him how awesome he was.

Anna: Had a meeting and lots of homework. Haven't seen it.

Caleb: You missed out. People are loving it.

Anna: I'm busy.

Caleb thought for a minute, then texted:

Caleb: Hey, you are super smart. Any ideas for a new show? I need something huge. Something that's never been reported before.

Anna: I can't predict what weird things people will believe. Do I look like a psychic? CU later.

Does she look like a psychic? Of course not. But, a psychic, huh? A psychic? YES! He knew Anna was smart, but this was genius. He was going to go see a psychic. He'd meet with someone who could predict his future, maybe tell a few ghost stories, and he could record the session and share it on his channel. His audience would eat it up!

Speaking of eating, Caleb remembered he was hungry. He grabbed the handle of the fridge and gave it a yank. He looked inside to find something to eat before starting his dreaded homework. He had no use for geometry, trigonometry, or numbers, in general, for that matter—unless those numbers were more followers. The addition of new viewers was definitely his kind of math.

As he snacked on some leftover pizza, Caleb pulled out his phone and searched the web for psychics in his area. He expected to find one or two, but shockingly found an entire page of people claiming to be able to tell his future. *Which one to pick?* Most of the names in the listing had reviews showing they were big zeros. Total scam artists. He kept scanning. *No. No. Nope, scammer.* He was about to give up when a name caught his eye. Agatha Dorsett. He knew that name. Agatha had been one of his grandmother's most trusted friends. If his grandmother trusted her, he could trust her too. Right?

Caleb decided not to wait on his big story. He needed to go right now. After reading her address again, he checked to make sure his phone was charged. Then he grabbed his bike and took off for Agatha's house. She lived pretty close by, so it wouldn't take him long to get there.

He arrived at Agatha's just before the sunset. Caleb practically bounced up the front steps. He straightened his clothes to have a neater appearance and raised his hand to knock on the door. Just before his knuckles touched the wood, the door opened.

"Hello," a crackly voice said. "How might I help you?"

Then he saw a tiny old woman open the door wider. It was Agatha Dorsett alright. He remembered her. With gray hair piled a mile-high on her head and wire-framed glasses, she was distinct and unforgettable.

"Ms. Dorsett, it's me. Caleb."

"Oh, Caleb, my dear child. How you have grown since I saw you last!" She clapped her hands together, clearly glad to see him. "I just finished making tea. Come in, come in."

The floor creaked as Caleb stepped through the hallway into a dimly lit kitchen. The house was old and so was the furniture. And, if he was being honest, it hadn't changed in years. Faded wallpaper with pink and yellow roses covered the walls. It looked like something out of a history book.

"Your grandmother and I used to have tea and biscuits every Thursday night. She was such a dear friend. We talked about a lot of things, but her favorite topic was you. She talked about you all of the time, you know."

"She talked about you too, ma'am. She enjoyed your company very much."

Agatha poured Caleb a thick brown tea and dropped a few sugar cubes into the cup.

She placed a plate of shortbread cookies on the table and lowered herself gently into her seat.

"We could talk all day about your grandmother. She was such a lovely woman. But that's not why you are here, is it?"

"No, ma'am," Caleb replied. "I have a ViewTube channel, and I report on the interesting and unusual things that happen in our town. Paranormal things."

"I'm sure I don't know what a ViewTube might be. But perhaps you can explain it to me."

"Yes, ma'am," Caleb said. "A ViewTube channel is just a place where I post videos that I make. I talk about some of the weird things that people see and do in our town. I've reported on bigfoot sightings, ghosts, even that time when Mr. Hendrickson tried to convince everyone that aliens were living in his guest room. A lot of people are interested in the stories I share."

He paused for a moment, gearing up to ask about what he came for. "I thought people might want to hear from someone who can predict the future. I thought that maybe you could share some stories with me and my audience. It might even help me to grow a larger audience."

Agatha tapped her long, wrinkled fingers on the table. She looked at the ceiling and closed her eyes. She breathed in deep breaths. She opened her eyes and stared right into Caleb's face.

"No," she said.

Wait . . . what?

But before Caleb could ask, Agatha began to talk.

"Something is coming, Caleb. Something sinister. Something scary. Something that will change this town, and not for the better." She reached out and patted Caleb's hand.

Caleb swallowed hard and stared at Agatha intently. Beads of sweat collected on his forehead and his clothes suddenly felt like they were choking him.

"What do you mean?" he asked. His foot tapped nervously under the table.

She continued, "A storm is coming. It

will be devastating. People will change. Are you listening?"

"Yes, ma'am, I am."

She continued talking. "One thing will remain constant. You must rely on a friend and trust in her. It will be the only thing that can save the town."

"Um, ok. I, um, ok." Caleb was shaken. He wasn't exactly sure what Agatha meant, but she seemed so serious.

"Go now," Agatha whispered. "You must get ready for the storm."

Caleb got up from his chair quickly. He almost tipped it over, but he caught it and set it right. He watched Agatha's face as he walked backward down the hall. Her voice had been so eerily calm. He tripped on the rug and fell into the wall on his way to the door. Agatha's dark eyes held his gaze so intently, following him until he was out the door. Caleb was scared. Shivers ran up and down his arms and goosebumps appeared, even though he didn't feel cold. He pulled the screen door closed quickly and had to hold onto the porch railing to keep from falling as he turned and stumbled down the steps.

Caleb went looking for a story, and
WHAM . . . it hit him hard. It was like a slap
in the face. He stood at the bottom of the
porch steps and looked out, trying to slow his
breathing, thinking about what Agatha said.
A pitch-black sky had settled over the town.
While the air up to now had been still, a light
wind started to blow. Small pockets of what
looked like heat lightning lit up the sky with
bright blasts of blinding white light. Caleb
quickly hopped on his bike and pedaled toward
home. As he pedaled, the winds began to blow

harder. As the winds blew harder, it felt like hands were pushing at him and he struggled to keep his bike upright. A light rain sprinkled down. Claps of thunder boomed so loud and strong that it felt like the ground was shaking beneath him.

By the time Caleb reached home, the rain was falling in huge droplets, splashing on the ground with great force. Blue, yellow, and orange lightning lit up the sky. The thunder continued louder and stronger; it shook the whole house as he carried the bike up the porch steps and brought it into the house. He leaned it against the wall in the entryway and bolted the front door.

Caleb walked to the front window and pulled back the curtain. As he looked out of the window, he saw the strong winds pick up a chair from his neighbor's porch and drop it in the street. It rolled and bounced until he could not see it anymore.

Plants were pulled out of the ground by the roots and spun and twirled in the air, showing him a strange and scary dance. Caleb had experienced storms before, but nothing like this. Running downstairs to take shelter in the basement, he felt safe until a huge bolt of lightning struck outside. Then everything went dark. Caleb held his breath. The silence was now deafening. He couldn't hear the rain or the thunder. When he finally let the air out of his lungs, that was the only thing he could hear.

Now what? The power was out, and his cell phone had no reception. Nothing. Silence. Caleb had never been more scared. While he was sitting on the basement floor, time seemed to stand still. Maybe because the AC was off, maybe because of his fear, Caleb felt unbearably hot and sweaty. Feeling like the worst of the storm had passed, he slowly went back upstairs. In the living room, he grabbed a magazine off the coffee table. He waved the paper in front of his face, hoping the movement of the air might cool him. He turned back and looked out the window. At just that moment, a loud crack of lightning lit up the sky. It struck a large tree in his neighbor's yard and caused a chain of sparks and pops. The trunk of the tree split and crashed to the ground, smashing down on top of his neighbor's car.

When are Mom and Dad getting home? He wondered. They'd gone out for dinner with friends. But where were they now?

It might have been twenty minutes. It might have been one hour. But the storm finally dissipated. Once he was sure that the wind had died down, he gathered his nerve, unlocked and then pulled open the front door. He cautiously stepped out onto the front porch. He thought he could survey the damage and see if any of his neighbors had power. That's when the howling started. Not just the usual cry of the coyotes that lived nearby. This was haunting. High pitched, almost sad sounding, and it seemed to go on forever. It wasn't just one voice either, but a symphony of voices layered one on top of the other like the mythical banshee's cry. Then it stopped, just like that. The power returned. Although the storm ended, a light rain still fell.

And that was when Caleb realized he had not recorded one single moment of it. Not one.

Caleb needed to talk to Anna. If anyone could help him understand this situation, it was her. He thought about what Agatha said. And how she had made it clear that he needed someone, someone he could trust. It had to be Anna. In spite of all their differences, she is the one person that had his back.

> Caleb: Can U meet me tomorrow?

5

Anna was actually interested in what Caleb
had to say. After last night's strange storm, she
needed to talk to someone. She always relied
on science to explain how things worked or
why things happened. Last night, too many
unexplained things took place. To start, she
had set up some equipment to measure the
wind speed and the precipitation. But none of
her equipment registered any activity. None.
She'd never experienced that before. Even with
the power out, she should have been able to
collect some data. It was weird how quickly the

storm began, how powerful it was, and then how it stopped so quickly. Then, of course, there was the unusual howling. Just thinking about it made her shiver. Now that it was over, she thought maybe her imagination was getting the best of her. There must be a logical explanation. Even if she hadn't figured it out yet.

When she arrived at Bee's Coffee Shop, Caleb was already there with her favorite coffee—hot and waiting, full of sugar and cream. It made her feel good that he could still be so thoughtful.

"Thanks for meeting me, Anna. I really need your help right now. Please just hear me out before you decide to argue with me. Please. Just keep an open mind."

Anna nodded her head and took a sip of her coffee.

"I went to see Agatha last night. Agatha Dorsett."

"Your grandmother's old friend? Why go to see her? Is she okay?"

"Did you know she is a psychic?" Caleb asked.

Anna choked on her coffee a bit and began coughing. She shook her head from side to side.

"Okay, so clearly you didn't know." Caleb continued, "You know I've been looking for another story. One that would wow my audience. Help to grow my presence, right?"

Anna just nodded her head, still recovering from her coffee mishap, wiping her mouth and the table, which was splattered with coffee.

"So, it was cool, but a little creepy. She just knows things. She told me about the storm before it happened. She told me that this is just the beginning. Even though the storm has passed, it isn't really over." Caleb stopped and looked at Anna.

"Oh, Caleb," Anna almost whispered. Then, she dissolved into a fit of laughter. Her head bobbed, shoulders shaking, and she grabbed her stomach as she continued to laugh out loud.

Caleb dropped his head, looking down at his shoes as Anna continued laughing.

Once her laughter died down, he spoke again. "Anna, you have been my friend forever.

We used to be so close. You are the only person in this town that can help me. Agatha predicted it. She said I would need you to save our town. Please, Anna, I need you."

The tightness and desperation in Caleb's voice caught Anna's attention. She felt a little sorry for laughing at him. She knew it had to be a big deal if he was asking for help from her. She just didn't believe what he was saying. A psychic prediction of doom? Come on. This was too much.

"Listen, Caleb, you are right. We have been friends for a long time. If I were in trouble or needed a friend, I would call you for sure. However, I just have a hard time believing in a seer of the future. I have studied the weather reports and listened to the news. The storm is over. The skies are clear. And, other than some relatively minor damage, everything is back to normal. Just look at this." Anna pulled up the local weather report and it showed the usual warm temperatures and no rainfall in the near future.

Scrolling through the reports, she didn't

find any other news reports of continued wild weather. The only reports showed some of the damage from the storm.

"I'm sorry you didn't get your big story this time, but I'm sure you will find another one soon. There is plenty of weirdness in this town," she said.

For dinner, Anna and her parents went to
the Foggy Creek Diner for meatloaf night.
The diner buzzed with people laughing and
talking. Tonight was special as the family
was celebrating Anna's conditional college
acceptance. She felt so good and was excited
to think about going away to college. The
idea of living in a dorm on campus, meeting
new people, and having access to a bigger lab
excited her.

    She gazed out the window of the diner,
expecting to see the usual bustle on Main

Street. Families shuffling in and out of the grocery store, running into the pharmacy to pick up a prescription, or stopping at the ice cream shop for a chocolate milkshake.

BAM!

Something hit the window with such force Anna thought the glass was going to shatter. A hairy, sharp-clawed creature was banging against the glass like it was trying to break through. It was making a horrible screeching sound and dripping a purplish foam from its mouth. She thought it resembled a rabbit, but she'd never seen one this aggressive or wild. Maybe it had rabies?

As quickly as it attacked the glass window, it flopped on the ground, then bolted down the street. The families in the diner were scared. Most people in the diner were frozen, clearly afraid to get up from their tables. A few guests took out their phones to try to video the beast. A few small children cried. Anna couldn't believe what she just saw. She had volunteered at the vet clinic last summer and knew animal behavior could be different when an animal was sick or scared. But, she had never seen anything like this before.

Anna texted her science club partner, Stephanie.

> **Anna:** I just saw something that I can't explain. Have you ever seen an animal with rabies?

> **Stephanie:** Nope. Read about it.

> **Anna:** I could have sworn what I saw was a rabbit, but it had these really sharp teeth and claws. Missing fur. Purple foamy mouth. Attacked the window at the diner.

> **Stephanie:** That is not rabies.

Down the road, Agatha Dorsett sat on her front porch—feeling like she was being watched. She closed her eyes and tried to get a visualization of what was happening. She sighed, knowing that her time was drawing near.

She stood up slowly and turned to look at her home. She wanted to remember every detail. She'd had such a good life here. She wished she was able to call Caleb, to tell him more, to tell him to be strong. She wanted to be able to say goodbye. She held that thought close and turned around just in time to see a drooling beast approach her porch and howl loudly. It was the last sound she heard.

Caleb's phone was blowing up. He couldn't keep up with all the messages. Strange beasts were roaming through town. Rabbits, coyotes, even a deer with patchy fur, sharp claws, and purple foam around the mouth had been spotted. They seemed to attack anything, from mailboxes and windows to small pets like cats and dogs. It seemed unbelievable, but they had even tried to bite a few residents. Not only were they scary and aggressive, but they were destroying people's property and damaging objects all over the town. Caleb got most of the calls because people thought maybe he could find out what was going on and he could report about the dangers.

Some townspeople sent him video clips. He viewed each clip carefully. Several people in town filmed different animals throwing themselves at objects or chasing after smaller animals. He tried to decide which of the clips were the best to post on his channel. It was hard though, because in all the videos, the animals exhibited similar behaviors, had the same mutations, and all seemed to be entering the main part of town from the same direction.

All of a sudden, Caleb realized something big. They all came into town from the west. They were coming from the direction of the sinkholes. Could that be the source of the problem? He decided to text Anna.

Caleb: Hey Anna. Have U heard about the animals?

Anna: yup.

Caleb: I've been watching videos . . . I think the source could be the sinkholes. Is that even possible?

Anna: I don't know how

Caleb: Come with me. Let's go check it out.

Anna: Don't know if that's a good idea, but ok. Meet you at 5 at school. I'll drive.

It all seemed so strange. The weather was beautiful and sunny, but there was a heaviness in the air. Clouds looked full of fear and uncertainty. As they drove through town, evidence of the storm seemed to be everywhere they looked. Some tree branches still littered the road, and household items were strewn about. Mailboxes had blown over. There were scrapes and claw marks on doors and on cars, proof that something was clearly wrong with the animals roaming in town. Gentle animals turned into aggressive beasts. Birds were attacking one another. Squirrels were ripping out their own fur.

"I hope I'm wrong, but it seems that the animals come into town from the same direction," Caleb said.

"I can't imagine what happened," Anna said as she shook her head.

As Anna drove slowly down the main road, a coyote ran next to the car. It looked normal, no weird markings or changes.

"Look, Caleb! A coyote. It looks like it's headed straight for the sinkholes."

She drove at a snail's pace until they approached the location of the sinkholes. Anna put the car in park.

"Anna, what is that?" Caleb asked as they stared in the direction of the sinkholes.

"I've never seen anything like this before."

They watched as purple mist rose around the sinkholes. They could see puddles of goop on the ground. The coyote slowly made its way into the mist. A sad howl filled the air, followed by a ferocious barking sound. Then, the coyote emerged. Changed. Its claws had grown long and pointy, clumps of hair were missing from all over its body, and a purple foam dripped from its large fangs.

The coyote leapt forward, all four feet forcefully landing on the hood of the car. It leered at Caleb and Anna through the window. As it stared into the vehicle, the coyote-beast pawed and scratched at the windshield. Its sharp claws digging into the paint, making a horrible scraping sound. It howled and barked. Purple slime dripped from its fangs as it bit at the window, trying desperately to get to Anna and Caleb. Anna's hands clutched the steering wheel. She was afraid.

"Caleb, what do we do? It's going to break through the glass," Anna yelled.

Caleb leaned over, honked the horn, and shouted, "Go away! Get out of here. Get!" Caleb covered Anna's head with his arms. "Brace for the worst in case the glass shatters!" The car rocked back and forth.

Just when it looked like the coyote was going to break through the window, it jumped down and took off toward the town. Caleb let go of Anna. Her heart raced. Finally, she released a long sigh.

"Are you okay?" Caleb asked Anna.

"I'm fine. But there is something I have to do and you aren't going to like it. I've got to collect some of that purple sludge. If I can test it, I might be able to figure out what it is," she said.

"I think that is a terrible idea. What if another monster comes along?"

"You'll just have to scare it off. We have got to try to figure out what this stuff is if we want to be able to control it."

"I'm going to repeat what I said. This is a terrible idea."

"Look in the trunk of the car. My golf clubs should be there. Grab a club in case you need a weapon to defend yourself," she told him. "I'm not sure it will do us any good, but at least it's something."

Anna gathered her equipment to go collect some of the slime. She tied a scarf around her mouth and nose to prevent breathing in the mist. Then she took a deep breath and marched away from the car.

As she was collecting the slime, she heard a wail that was half scream and half cry. A figure appeared from the mist. The figure looked almost like Bobby, the star of the baseball team. But he did not look human. His blue eyes had turned purple. Bobby spent a lot of time in the sun at baseball practice, so he always looked tan. But now, his skin was paler, almost translucent. His face was expressionless. Anna had never believed in zombies, but standing right in front of her was a zombie. It walked right past Anna's car and headed back toward the town.

After the zombie was far enough away from her, Anna ran back to the car.

"What just happened?" Caleb asked as she jumped in.

Before she could answer, there were more cries, more wailing. And several other people emerged from the mist, changed, just like Bobby.

The zombies began shuffling toward the car.

"There are more!" Anna yelled. She tossed the slime specimens into the back seat.

She started the engine, hit the gas, and sped away from the zombies.

9

Anna couldn't believe what she just witnessed. *What caused Bobby to turn into a zombie? When did the other townspeople enter and what in the world happened to them? Why was this happening? Why? Why?*

"We have got to keep people away from the mist," Caleb said.

"You have to broadcast. Tell your followers to stay away. They will listen to you. They trust you. People need to be warned and they need to stay indoors for safety."

"Come on the show with me. Let's talk about what we saw."

"I'm not even sure what I saw," Anna said. "But, okay, let's do it."

Anna drove to the high school. It was hard to think clearly about all of this. None of it made any scientific sense. Not the psychic prediction. Not the animal behavior, and certainly not people changing in front of her eyes. This was bad. Really bad.

"Cover your nose and mouth with this," Anna said, tossing a windbreaker to Caleb. "Don't stop running until you get to the office door."

Beating on the office door, Anna yelled, "Open up! Help! Let us in!"

"We're trying to fight the zombies!" Caleb yelled.

The night janitor, Mr. Gee, threw open the door. He waved his hands at them and said, "Get in, get in. There are zombies all over town!" After helping them get inside, he locked the door behind them.

Anna and Caleb ran to the studio. Once

they entered the studio, Caleb prepared the lights and sound for the broadcast. He handed Anna a headset and put one on himself. Then he tested the audio and video feed. Anna took a deep breath, and Caleb turned on the camera.

"Hey there friends, fellow students, and followers of the bizarre. It's me, Caleb Henderson, and have I got a story for you. But, first, let me introduce my guest. Most of you know her as our local science expert and president of the science club, but if you don't know her, meet Anna Campos. Anna and I just came back from a scary adventure. I don't recommend it to anyone. Based on the number of calls and messages you all have sent, I'm thinking that most of you have probably seen the unusual beasts roaming around town. Patches of missing fur, sharp teeth, long claws, strange howls and barks. These beasts have been on the loose in town, attacking both human and non-human targets. Only minor injuries have been reported so far. That is until now. It seems that some of our neighbors and friends are also showing signs of strange behavior.

Anna and I witnessed people coming out of a purple mist down by the sinkholes. People are not the same after breathing the mist. They look and act like zombies. Will they become aggressive like the animals? Let's hope not. In order to stay safe, please stay indoors. I repeat, please stay indoors. Anna, anything to add?"

Anna thought for a moment and looked directly into the camera. "Please. I know this sounds unbelievable, but it's all true. There is a mist that is unsafe to breathe. You must avoid it at all costs. Stay in your homes. Keep your windows closed. Lock your doors. Keep yourself, your families, and your pets indoors and safe until this problem passes. Please. Listen to us. Stay away from the purple mist and stay away from the sinkholes."

"You heard it from the expert. Stay home. Stay indoors. Stay safe. We will report back as soon as we can with more information. Be safe, friends! We're out!"

"We have to get the word to the local news teams. Maybe the police can put up barriers or blockades to keep people away from the sinkholes until we can figure out what is happening and how to stop it."

"I'm on it, Anna. Calling the police and the news now. And I'll update my pages too."

Once the warning had been broadcast, Caleb closed up the studio. Anna reached out and grabbed Caleb's hand and held on tight as they walked out toward her car. Once outside, they walked in silence. Anna wondered what to do and planned what the next steps might be. The parking lot looked deserted. Deep in thought, Anna almost missed a math teacher, Mrs. Carp, walking toward them. Maybe not walking so much as plodding slowly. Her eyes had the purple hue and her skin was pasty white. She looked like she was in a daze. They froze.

"Caleb, hurry."

Anna pulled Caleb behind a bush. They waited and watched as the teacher slowly walked through the parking lot. Mrs. Carp didn't seem like she had a purpose or a specific direction. Instead, she wandered through the parking lot and stopped outside the front entrance to the school. She just stood there, staring.

"Caleb, let's go. Now," Anna whispered.

Anna pulled Caleb out from their hiding place and they rushed over to her car.

"Look on the ground." Anna pointed to a small patch of purple goop, almost like a trail behind the teacher's path. "I need to collect some of that stuff so I can analyze it."

"Don't get any of it on your skin."

She grabbed her bag from the car. Then she carefully put on latex gloves and pulled out an overly large cotton swab and a small jar. Scraping as much of the goop as she could gather, she put the sample in the jar. She tightened the lid. Then she took out another jar and dropped the cotton swab and the latex gloves into it for safekeeping. After she finished, she ran back to her car. Caleb was waiting in the passenger's seat.

"Now, we can try to see what we are dealing with," she said.

Anna dropped Caleb off at his house and went home. She lay awake for a long time that night wondering what the purple stuff could be and why the people and animals changed. She wished she had more equipment at home to test the substance tonight, but she needed the lab. After rolling around uncomfortably for a while, Anna threw the covers off her legs and went to the window. She just needed to think. Looking into the night sky might help her to relax. Then she heard the otherworldly sounds.

When she opened the curtains and pulled

them to the side, she could see the street from
her window. She was instantly alarmed at
how many zombie people could be seen just
wandering. There were howls and shrieks
coming from the strange beasts. She watched
in horror as one of the smaller beasts sunk
its teeth into the leg of one of the zombies.
It seemed like the zombie felt nothing. It
just stood there while the beast drew blood.
She put her hand over her mouth and gasped
loudly. Panicking, she began to shake. Was it
possible that one of these beasts might get into
her bedroom? Anna wasn't taking any chances.
She looked around her room frantically and
got the idea of barricading herself in the room.
Then she grabbed the edge of her bookcase
and pulled it to block the window. She grabbed
her desk chair and wedged it under the
doorknob and piled books high on top, hoping
it would keep any intruders out. Deciding she
felt safest leaving the lights of her bedroom on,
she crawled back into bed and pulled the covers
up under her chin.

Where were her parents?

Anna: Mom! Are you home?

Anna: DAD! Where are you?

Minutes, then hours ticked by. No response from either her mom or her dad. *Had they turned into zombies?*

The next morning, Anna awoke to a frantic knocking on the front door.

"Mom! You home? Mom! Are you going to get that?" Anna yelled from her room. "Dad, can you hear me?"

The house was quiet. No sign of her parents. She checked her phone. Still no response from her texts.

"I'm coming," Anna called out. "Just a minute."

She dressed quickly in jeans and a T-shirt and took down the pile of books from the chair. She moved the chair out of the way and opened the door, peeking her head out and pausing to take a quick look down the hallway. It looked clear, so she hustled down the stairs and looked out the front window. A woman Anna had never seen stood on the porch. Dressed in a brown suit jacket and matching pants, the woman looked professional but also a little out of place. And she looked very nervous. Anna opened the door a crack.

"Hello," the woman said. "I'm looking for Anna Campos. Are you her?"

"Yes, I'm Anna," she replied, relieved that the person on her porch was not ghostly pale and had dark brown eyes instead of purple.

"Hi, Anna. I'm Dr. Sarah Ebright. We had a meeting scheduled for this morning." Dr. Ebright looked uncomfortable and kept glancing around as she stood on the porch.

Anna opened the door wide. "I am so sorry, Dr. Ebright," Anna said. "With all the craziness going on in this town, I completely forgot that you were coming."

"I heard the news about the after effects of the storm on my way into town. It seemed, well, it seemed made up. Like a prank or fake news. I thought there had to be a reasonable explanation for what was being reported.

But, then, I saw the zombies . . ." Her voice drifted off.

Of all the times for a college interview, Anna thought. Then, to settle her anxiety, she told herself that it was time to act like a professional scientist. *Facts, objective facts. Time to remain reasonable and, above all, rational.*

"Can I get you a cup of tea, Dr. Ebright? It sounds like you could use one," Anna said. Then she turned, locked the door, and slid a heavy coffee table in front of the door for added safety. As Anna pulled the curtains closed, she tried to sound calm. "This should help keep us safe and protect us from them."

Dr. Ebright sighed in relief. "Tea would be lovely, thank you." Dr. Ebright cleared her throat and asked, "Where are your parents?"

Biting down on her lower lip, Anna tried to hold back a cry, "I . . . I don't know."

Anna went to the kitchen. Dr. Ebright followed her and sat down at the kitchen table. While making tea, Anna described the details of the strange storm that rolled through town, followed by the events surrounding the sinkholes and the mist. She talked about the changes to people and to the animals. She couldn't believe what she was saying to the professor.

Dr. Ebright listened closely.

"After the incident with the zombies on the street, I saw news reporters everywhere. They had on gas masks, like the ones you see in old sci-fi movies. I'm not sure I've ever seen so many microphones, cameras, and news vans," Anna said.

Anna went on to describe Caleb's visit to the psychic and his ViewTube reporting. "What do you think, Dr. Ebright? What should we do next?"

Dr. Ebright took out her phone. She typed furiously for a few minutes, and then looked at Anna.

"Okay, here is what I think. We need some serious brainstorming. I just messaged a friend of mine who happens to study paranormal activity. I hope you don't mind, but I invited her to your house."

"That is great," Anna said. "What else do we do?"

"Call your friends. Is there anyone in the science club that might be able to join us? Who lives close by? I think we are going to need a team of people to figure out how to handle the mist, the people, and the animals who have seemed to change."

Anna nodded and said, "On it." She texted Caleb and a few members of the science club.

> Anna: EMERGENCY!!!!!!!!!!!!!! MEET AT MY HOUSE.

She paused and then texted again.

> Anna: But ONLY if you can get here safely. WATCH OUT FOR THE ZOMBIES!!!!

While they waited for the rest of the team to arrive, Anna and Dr. Ebright turned on the news. It was strange to see the reporters telling the news while wearing gas masks and hazmat suits. They reported from the school, from the diner, from the football fields, and from the front yards of different residents of the town. Anna was sure Caleb would be excited because some of the reporters were joined by paranormal investigators. They, too, seemed to be on every corner. While the number of people visiting could help spread awareness of the problem, Anna thought about something else. *More people could mean more infected people breathing in the mist. Then they would have more zombies. Would the protective gear be enough to keep them safe?* She shook her head. *What were they going to do?*

Caleb and Stephanie arrived at Anna's house, prepared to brainstorm ideas. Anna reached out to a few other club members to join the team, but they were too scared to leave their homes. It was probably for the best anyway. She didn't want to risk any more lives.

The kitchen table was piled high with notebooks, pens, and a variety of snacks. Each member of the team had their own tablet or laptop. They needed to keep an eye on the local news and to be able to research as needed.

Anna downloaded maps of the town and

of the sinkholes. While busy researching and planning, she was surprised to hear another knock at the door. Anna peeked outside to see a figure with a long dark coat carrying a large backpack. The person at the door wore dark, heavy eyeliner and deep blue lipstick. Her hair fell past her shoulders, dyed at the ends a royal blue color. Not sure if she should let the visitor in, Anna just stared at her. Finally, the woman knocked again, causing Anna to jump. Then Dr. Ebright came to the door. She smiled a big smile, opened the door, and said, "It's okay. This is my friend, Margot Sheffield. She studies the paranormal. I invited her to join us."

After sighing in relief, Anna said, "Welcome. We are so happy to have you here."

Caleb stared at Margot Sheffield, the legendary Margot Sheffield.

"I can't believe you are here. I can't, I mean I can, I mean, hi. I have been following you for years." Caleb stuttered. He was totally starstruck. "I modeled my ViewTube channel after yours. I hope that's okay. Your show is, well, it's so good. I mean, great. I mean, hi." Caleb felt himself blush.

Margot laughed. "Hello there, Caleb. I'd know you anywhere. I have followed you for a while. It's nice to finally meet you," she said.

Caleb blushed again. Then he took Margot's hand and shook it up and down. The whole time he grinned like a fool.

"Okay, Caleb. Let go of the poor woman's hand and let's get to work. You can stare at Margot while we are working," Anna said. She shook her head and laughed.

Caleb took a seat next to Margot. He could not stop smiling.

That is, he grinned until a loud thud on the front window reminded him of the serious situation raging on outside of the house. Caleb turned and looked at the front window. He could see a beast throwing itself against the window. It howled and shrieked, drooling purple slime. He thought for sure it was going to break through.

Anna ran toward the window, a golf club in her hand. "Just in case it breaks the glass and gets in," she whispered.

But, as quickly as the attack started, it stopped. And the beast took off down the street.

"As you can see, we have a huge problem on our hands. We have to find a solution," Anna said. "Let's get to work." She put the golf club down.

Caleb noticed how Anna's hands were shaking. She was terrified. So was he. But he knew she was trying so hard to appear calm. To Work. To focus on the work and the objective science.

Dr. Ebright, Anna, Caleb, Margot, and Stephanie finally sat down to get started. "Okay, team, I want to thank you all for coming," Anna began. "The problem is this mist and the ooze, and we need to figure out what it is and how we get rid of it."

"We also need to figure out what to do with the animals and people who have been affected by the mist," Caleb added. "I know this is scary, but there has to be something we can do."

"I have reached out to colleagues of mine and, so far, no one has experienced anything like this before," said Dr. Ebright. "So, we have a unique problem and need to find a unique solution. Let's go back to the beginning and see if we can figure this out."

"Well, okay," Caleb started. Then he told them about Agatha Dorsett, her psychic prediction, and the weird, wild storm.

"She knew a storm was coming, that it was going to bring evil to town and that Anna and I needed to work together to try to help the town survive." Caleb paused his story and shifted in his chair.

Anna continued, "None of my equipment worked in the storm. Nothing. Then, just as suddenly as the storm started, it stopped." Anna picked at her fingernails. Caleb knew she did this when she was agitated.

"That's when the beasts appeared," she said. "I was having dinner at the diner, and I thought one of the beasts was going to break through the glass. I was so scared. So was everyone in the diner. Then, Caleb realized the animals coming into town were coming from the direction of the sinkholes, so we decided to check it out," Anna said. "We got a front-row view of what happens when a person or animal breathes in the mist. They change."

"It would make sense that the mist is causing the changes. There must have been some type of chemical reaction that affected the air around the sinkholes. The change takes place once someone breathes in the mist," Dr. Ebright pointed out.

"I agree," said Anna. "We just need to find out what that reaction is and how we can reverse it."

"That is going to be really hard to do without having a sample to work with," Dr. Ebright said with a sigh. "That would have been helpful, but after that creature just appeared out of nowhere, I really don't feel comfortable sending any of us out into the streets to try and collect a sample."

"Your bag!" Caleb shouted.

Anna's face lit up. She clapped her hands together and smiled. "Then we are in luck," she said. "I happen to have a sample in my bag."

"Well then," Dr. Ebright said. "Now all we need is a lab."

Anna gathered their belongings, including scarves to wrap around their faces. "Let's take two vehicles," she suggested. "In case we need to separate later."

Driving slowly down the street to avoid the debris and zombie-like people, Anna noticed that most of the stores and shops in town were closed up tight. The front window of Bee's Coffee Shop had a huge crack in the glass. Someone had taped the window back together with silver electrical tape.

It would have to hold until the trouble passed,

she thought. The damage from the storm still needed to be cleaned up, but that would also have to wait too. Right now, the only objective was to find out how to get rid of the mist. And the zombies.

"Here we are," Caleb said as he got out of the car. "I hope this works."

"I think you need to go to the studio. Keep sending out warnings and ask people to let you know what they see," Anna said. "Take Margot with you. Maybe she can help. I'll take Stephanie and Dr. Ebright to the lab and we'll get to work."

"You've got this. I believe in you," Caleb said.

Anna smiled and put her hand on Caleb's arm. "Thank you. That means a lot. I believe in you too."

He asked, "You ready? We need to make a run for it."

"Let's go," she said.

Zombie people wandered through the parking lot of the high school. Occasionally, a hairy animal with sharp fangs zoomed through the parking lot and repeatedly threw itself into a parked car or against the school walls.

Caleb, Anna, and the rest of the team ran toward the building. This time, the door was unlocked. There was no sign of Mr. Gee, the janitor. Had the zombies gotten him?

"To the studio! To broadcast!" Anna shouted and pointed at Caleb and Margot. "Dr. Ebright and Stephanie, come with me! To the lab!"

Caleb burst into the studio with Margot following close behind.

"I think if we reach out to all of our followers, we should be able to spread the message for people to stay indoors. We should also ask them to share what they see. We can make a map to track the information and be able to pinpoint the biggest trouble spots in town," Caleb said.

"That sounds like a good plan," Margot replied.

Caleb watched as Margot picked up a headset and immediately started broadcasting.

He got some paper and markers and began sketching out the main streets and buildings in town. As Margot's followers shared what they could see, Caleb added the information to the map. Then it was his turn.

"Hey there, friends, fellow students, and followers of the bizarre. It's me, Caleb Henderson, and I want to keep you posted about the dangers here in Foggy Creek. I said it before, but let me say it again. Please stay indoors. It is not safe to leave your homes. Keep listening and checking for my posts. I will tell you if it is safe to go out. In the meantime, if you can see out your windows, let me know where you are and what you can see. This is important friends, our town is depending on us. Stay safe, my friends. I'm out."

With both Caleb and Margot's broadcasts complete, they shifted their focus to the map. They added the locations of the animals and zombie people that their followers shared with them. People also left comments that told them about the progress of the first responders. It was a relief to know that the police blocked access to the sinkholes.

On the other side of the school, Dr. Ebright called out to assign jobs and gather supplies. "Stephanie, find some blank slides and get the microscopes set up. Anna, we need beakers and Bunsen burners to test the compound combinations. Oh! Get the laptop ready so we can keep track of the tests that we run."

They bustled through the lab. Everyone was focused. Everyone tested, and everyone worked silently. The seriousness of the situation weighed down on them. The team worked for hours. As they developed the different compounds, they dropped those solutions on a sample of the purple slime. Each time, they held their breath hoping that they got the combination right. Each time, they were disappointed. Time was running out and so was the slime.

"Someone is going to have to go outside

soon and see if we can get another sample. I know it's not safe, but I don't know what else to try," Stephanie said.

Anna was trying to concentrate. Her frustration was at an all-time high. There was one sample left and she was using her last combination. If it didn't work, she wasn't sure anything would. Anna placed the last ooze sample in a dish and picked up a dropper. Then she pulled the solution up into the tube, held it over the dish, and gave it a good squeeze. She waited. And waited.

"It didn't work," she sighed. Anna put her head down on the table and closed her eyes. *What were they going to do?*

"Look," Dr. Ebright said quietly and pointed at the dish. Anna lifted her head and then looked at the dish. It was empty.

"You did it! Your solution made the ooze disappear," Dr. Ebright said. They had an answer to their problem! Anna couldn't have felt prouder of herself. She stood taller and let out a breath she didn't know she had been holding.

"Anna, how did you do it?" Stephanie asked.

"I have to admit, I'm curious too," Dr. Ebright added.

"Well," Anna started, "I remembered that in one of our club meetings, we were testing the stability of different compounds, so I dug out my notes. The one thing that continued to create changes to the compound was salt. I figured out that adding a little sodium chloride, table salt, to the chemical compound could destroy a bond. So, I tried it. The added salt broke the bond of the slime." Anna was beaming.

"Great thinking Anna," Dr. Ebright said. Now that we have a working compound, we need to make more of it."

"That's right, Dr. Ebright," Anna said. "We need to make more. A lot more."

Anna texted Caleb:

Anna: We got it. Come now. Hurry!

Anna and Stephanie got busy. They worked to create a liquid salt to squirt to get rid of the slime. Then, they filled every container in the lab and hoped it would be enough.

Caleb and Margot ran to the lab. They

could barely fit into the room with all the containers stacked up. Caleb looked around.

"I hate to be negative, but what do we do with all this stuff?" he asked.

He saw everyone in the room look stunned. Here they had a compound that could neutralize the ooze and hopefully dissolve the mist, but how were they going to deliver it?

"How about we use a plane and spray the solution over the town?" Stephanie asked.

"Great idea. But I don't know where we will find a plane and are you a pilot? Because we don't have one of those either," Caleb said.

"Oh, right. I'll keep thinking."

"Let's use sprinklers and spray everything with that," she suggested.

"Also, a great idea," Anna said. "I don't know that we can get the solution into the water supply or if that is a safe thing to do."

"I wish my dad were here," Stephanie said. "He's a firefighter and he always knows what to do. I'll text him."

Caleb put his hand on his neck and rubbed it, trying to release some of the tension.

"I don't know what a firefighter could do," he said.

"Unless . . ." Anna said. "Unless he's the driver. Stephanie, can your dad drive the fire engine?"

"He sure can," she replied.

"That's it!" Caleb exclaimed. He remembered that the town had one of the old-time fire engines that had the water tank attached to the truck. No hydrant would be necessary to fill the hose with water. It would be perfect!

"We add the solution to the water tank. Hook up the fire hose. And spray the mist. It should make the mist disappear," Anna practically shouted at the team.

"He's at work today. I'll text him now and ask him to meet us here," Stephanie said. Then she typed out a text.

"That takes care of the mist at the sinkholes. But what about the animals and people in town?" Anna exhaled. "This is never going to work."

Caleb was silent, racking his brain to figure out a solution.

"I've got it!" Caleb said. "Water Wars."

"I'm sorry. But I have no idea what you are talking about," said Dr. Ebright.

"Water Wars is something that happens at the end of every school year. The seniors get into teams, and everybody gets a super soaker. You know, those extra-large squirt guns? If you get soaked, you are out of the game. In this case, we put some of the solution into the water guns. We soak the people and animals and, hopefully, we reverse the process."

"That is just ridiculous enough to work," Margot said. "Nice thinking, Caleb."

Caleb beamed from the compliment.

"Now, we need to make a plan. What do we do first? How are we going to know where the trouble spots are?" Anna asked.

"I think somebody needs to stay in the studio and monitor the news. We need to stay in communication with everyone, including the police," Caleb said. The team looked at each other and all began talking at the same time.

Finally, Dr. Ebright spoke up.

"Listen, I don't know if I'm the best person for running around town and chasing these beasts. I am the oldest person here. I think I would be the most useful staying behind and monitoring the police and news channels. I can keep you all informed about where to track down the trouble."

Caleb agreed with Dr. Ebright. She would stay at the school and continue tracking. That way, she could direct the team where to find the people and animals that needed rescuing. She could also stay in touch with any needed first responders and the news outlets.

Once that had been decided, Caleb helped Anna and Stephanie as they transported the containers of the solution to the front of the school. Stephanie's dad and a crew of firefighters met them there, and they loaded the solution into the back of the truck.

First step . . . tackle the sinkholes.

Lights flashing and sirens blaring, the fire engine sped through town, eventually stopping close to the sinkholes. They could see the mist but felt relieved that no people or animals could be seen nearby. Stephanie's dad handed each person a gas mask to prevent them from breathing in any of the mist. He hooked up the hose to the tank and attached it to the truck.

Anna poured the solution, one container after another, into the tank. Margot, Caleb, Stephanie, and Anna lined up to hold onto the hose with the fire crew.

"So, how does this work?" Anna asked.

"Good question, Anna," said Stephanie's dad. "Once I turn on the water, it will very quickly flow into the hose. It creates a great deal of force, so you are going to have to hold on with both hands. It is going to be hard to control, but you have to keep a tight grip. Everybody understand?"

It was going to be a test of strength to make this happen, Anna thought.

Anna watched as Caleb used his heels to notch a secure spot in the ground. "So you don't slip and fall."

Grasping the hose tightly, Anna was as

ready as she could be. She also dug into the dirt with her heels, hoping to keep stable once the water started to flow.

"Okay, here goes," Stephanie's dad said. The water rushed through the hose with a tremendous amount of force. Anna struggled to keep control of the hose. They used all their might to aim the hose at the mist and hoped for the best, but Anna felt like they were losing control. The hose pulled her arms away from her body and she felt her hands slip and slide. Her feet dragged in the dirt as the hose pulled her from side to side.

"I don't know how much longer I can hang on," Anna said.

"You have to hang on," Caleb responded. "Don't let go. This has to work."

With her arms aching and legs burning, Anna continued to hang on as the hose sprayed. At first, it looked like nothing was happening. Just thousands of gallons of water spraying into the sky. The team held on and continued to move the hose back and forth into the mist.

"There isn't much left in the tank," Stephanie's dad yelled. "Isn't something supposed to be happening here?" he asked.

The team held on tight, trying to not be discouraged. Stephanie started to cry. Anna was exhausted, her arms and legs hurt, but she held onto the hose anyway. She felt like she had been holding on for hours when it had probably only been about five minutes. It was hard to say how long they sprayed, but soon the solution completely doused the mist. At last, the entire fog of purple mist disappeared. The sky looked clear. With the little solution they had left, they sprayed the ground around the sinkholes to be sure to destroy the ooze, too.

"Well, you did it, kids. If I hadn't seen it for myself, I'm not sure I would have believed it," Stephanie's dad said.

When the purple mist was completely gone, Anna dropped the hose. Her limbs were shaking, and her energy was spent, but there was so much more to do.

They got back in the truck and sped toward town.

The next step—Water Wars.

The team went by the school and found the collection of super soakers that had been collected for Water Wars. They loaded up the cars and drove to Main Street.

"We need to find a source of water to mix with the solution," Caleb said.

"Outside of the diner there are two water spigots," Anna said.

"Let's use the diner as home base, then," he said. He waved to Stephanie and Margot in the other car, signaling to them to park by the diner.

"Fill up the super soakers with the solution. Margot, get the perfect amount of water in them," he said. "Stephanie, make sure the caps are on tight."

"I think it makes sense for one of us to be in charge of refilling the soakers," Margot said. "Why don't I take charge of that. I'll soak anything that comes into this area, but I'll also keep watch behind you to fill the soakers as you empty them."

"Great idea, Margot. Everybody ready?" Caleb asked.

Each of the kids loaded up and carried several of the water guns. They approached Main Street and stood shoulder to shoulder, hearts racing but hopes high.

"Stephanie, you take the right side of the street. Anna, you take the left. I will head straight down the middle," Caleb said. "Aim for any part of the body where skin is showing. Soaking clothing might not be enough."

"Sounds good. When your gun empties, drop it and keep moving forward. Margot will pick up the empties and refill them. Meet back at the diner when you need to refill," Anna added.

"Ready?" Caleb asked.

Anna and Stephanie nodded.

"Good luck, everyone," said Anna.

Caleb and Stephanie started walking down the street. They turned their heads from side to side and adjusted their positions to see what was happening all around them.

"Do not fall victim to a sneak attack," he shouted to Stephanie.

As they walked through town, they soaked anybody that they could find.

Anna found a great spot outside of the coffee shop and waited behind a post. She watched the grocery store owner emerge from his shop. Pale white, purple-eyed, he walked in her direction. She waited until he was close, then let loose. She scored a direct hit. The solution hit him right in the face. He brought his hands up and wiped at his eyes. He shook his head and seemed to wake up. He blinked and Anna could see his eyes were blue. His skin lost its pale, ghostly hue. One down, many to go.

She continued moving down the street in the same way, blasting any person that crossed her path. On the other side of the street, Stephanie seemed to be having the same good luck. Anna saw her aim, fire, and, one by one, the zombies changed.

As the solution hit the skin of the zombies, the people of town seemed to snap out of their daze. Their skin returned to its healthy color and their purple eyes returned to their natural color. Anna knew they were making progress. She felt encouraged as she watched one person after another change back from their zombie state. Anna looked down the street and saw a man and woman stumbling clumsily. She headed in their direction and stopped suddenly. She recognized the dress the woman was wearing. That dress belonged to her mother.

"Mom! Dad! Is that you?" she yelled. The couple continued to walk. Anna ran up to them and stood right in their way. She took aim and sprayed the couple. She watched as they shook a little, rubbed their hands on their faces, and their normal skin color returned. Anna smiled and jumped at her parents. They held on tight as they hugged.

"Oh, Anna," her mom said. "I don't know what just happened. How did we get here?"

"I'll explain it all later," Anna said. "I'm just so happy that I found you."

Anna walked her parents to the diner. She noticed that people, like her parents, who had changed back, didn't know what had happened or why they were wandering through town.

They all seemed so happy to be alive, though. Neighbors waved to neighbors and embraced as they tried to figure out what was going on.

"Mom and dad, I want you to stay here at the diner. I will be back as soon as I can. You'll be safe here." Her parents nodded and agreed to stay put. Anna looked around as she headed back out to continue her work, saving the town. "What a mess," she said out loud. The town was a wreck. She saw broken glass littering the sidewalks. Doors and cars bore the scratches and tears of the wild animals that clawed at them. Tree limbs remained broken and visible on the streets. She was stunned, but couldn't stop to think about it now. There was still work to do.

Finding the zombie people was the easier part of the mission, Anna thought. *Now to find the animals.* That was going to be more challenging. She texted Caleb.

> Anna: We need more help. Can you reach out to your followers?

Caleb: I can try.

Caleb opened the video on his phone and recorded a quick message to his channel. "Hey there friends, fellow students, and followers of the bizarre. It's me, Caleb Henderson, and I need your help. Are you ready for a challenge? Grab your squirt guns and meet us on Main Street, in front of the diner. Look for my friend Margot. She will get you loaded up and ready to hunt. It's time to rid the town of these wild beasts. We'll be waiting. Stay safe, my friends. I'm out."

Once he finished posting, Caleb texted Anna.

Caleb: I'm going to head back to the diner and help Margot direct our new recruits. Is that okay with you?

Anna: Good idea. We'll be alright. Stephanie and I will keep going.

Caleb took off to the diner to help fill the guns with the extra solution and to direct all extra team members on what to do as the girls continued through the town, hunting the wild beasts.

Back at the school, Dr. Ebright communicated with the police and news outlets. She shared locations where zombies and animals had been spotted. With guidance from Dr. Ebright, the team knew where to track the rest of the people and the animals, and they were prepared to spray them all.

Anna felt powerful. She approached each animal carefully and doused it with the solution. She watched as one after another, the animals changed back. They still showed missing patches of fur, but the terrible fangs and claws disappeared. Most of them looked confused, then scampered away.

She called Caleb. "Hey, how's it going over there?"

"I can't believe how many people showed

up. This is great. We should have this done in no time," Caleb answered.

While Anna and Caleb continued to talk, Anna forgot about the danger. She didn't see a coyote, frothing with purple foam on its mouth, grumbling quietly, approach her from the right. The coyote growled and lunged, knocking Anna to the ground. Anna screamed and dropped her phone. Not only that, but she dropped her super soaker.

The coyote bit at her leg as she kicked at the animal. She rolled away and grabbed the water gun. Then she turned back and sprayed the coyote. He lay down at her feet and whined softly. His beastly appearance softened until he no longer looked quite so dangerous. Then he ran away.

Anna lay back on the ground and took a deep breath. She was fine. The coyote hadn't broken through her skin. That is, she was fine until Caleb came running over and about squashed her as he tried to check and see if she was okay.

"Caleb, let go of me. You are squishing me."

"You screamed! And fell. I thought that beast got you. I'm so glad you are okay," Caleb whispered.

"Me too, Caleb. Me too."

It took some time, but the team was able to
soak every person and animal that needed
to be changed back to its original form.
The empty solution containers and super
soakers were abandoned in a pile out front
of the diner. They would be recycled later.
The owner of the diner invited everyone to
come in for a sandwich, a glass of lemonade,
and to just be together. Stories needed to be
told, and people needed to fill in the gaps
from the time they lost when they weren't
themselves. The news trucks and paranormal

investigators interviewed the residents about what they could remember. Once the residents finished sharing their stories and the reporters collected their information, the trucks packed up and moved on to find another story in another town.

Caleb thought it would be a good idea to talk to his followers. He needed to thank them for their help and give them an update.

"Hey there, friends, fellow students, and followers of the bizarre. It's me, Caleb Henderson. I'm streaming live here in front of the Foggy Creek Diner. Most of the residents of our town are gathered here to tell their stories. We have survived. Thanks to those of you who showed up to help, and I'm grateful for all you believers out there. This might just be the most remarkable thing that has ever happened here in our town. Check my channels for video footage and tales of the bizarre. If you have a story to tell, please send it my way. Stay safe, friends. I'm out." Caleb was so relieved that the danger had passed.

Margot approached Caleb. "When I got up this morning, I had no idea that my day was going to be this interesting. I think you have a great future."

He smiled and nodded his head. "I appreciate that. I still can't explain why or how this all happened," he said. "But I am glad that I was able to meet you, and I can't thank you enough for coming and helping us out."

Caleb and Margot shook hands.

"Caleb, you know how to build a following and you have a great flair for reporting. What are you planning to do next? A degree in paranormal studies or communications?"

"I've never thought college was for me," he said. "But, after this, I'm wondering if it might be in my future after all." Caleb shrugged and smiled. He had a lot of thinking to do. Maybe being more like Anna wouldn't be so bad. He might be able to continue connecting with people. Caleb looked around to try to find Anna. He saw she was deep in conversation with Dr. Ebright.

"Well, Anna, I can honestly say that this is the most intense interview I have ever conducted," Dr. Ebright said. "I have traveled the country to find the best and brightest students to join our program at Tech. You were in my top twenty, but after this experience, after seeing your quick thinking and your skill in the lab, you have jumped to the top of the list as my number one candidate. I would like to offer you a spot in our biochemistry department. And, if you will agree to work as my teaching assistant, I would like to offer you a full scholarship, tuition and housing included. What do you say?"

Anna stared at Dr. Ebright. Tears ran down her cheeks as she nodded her head yes. A smile spread across her face and her eyes crinkled in the corners. She clasped her hands together and almost bounced on the balls of her feet. She felt like turning cartwheels. "Dr. Ebright, I would be honored to be your assistant and thank you so much for the scholarship. I can't thank you enough."

Dr. Ebright said her goodbyes, promised to get in touch with Anna soon, got in her car and drove away.

Caleb felt good as he watched the people of Foggy Creek. Eventually, the food ran low and the energy in the crowd decreased, so families started to head home. Caleb listened to discussions about how to clean up the town. The residents agreed to meet the next day to come up with a plan for putting the town back together.

Caleb watched Anna. When she turned and saw him looking, she grinned and ran toward him. They laughed out loud and hugged tightly. Anna shared her good news, and Caleb shared that he might have changed his plans.

Anna offered to help Caleb with applications if he decided to go to college.

"I think I'm going to head out to Agatha's house to make sure she knows everything is okay now. I mean, she is a psychic, so she probably already knows, but I want her to hear it from me. She was right, about all of it. Do you want to go with me?"

Anna looked at Caleb. "I'm sorry Caleb, but we can't go out to see Agatha."

She spoke softly. "I overheard the sheriff talking to some of our neighbors. Agatha didn't make it. She was the only person who didn't make it through this storm. I'm so sorry."

Then he shook his head and sighed. He couldn't believe it. Caleb put his head on Anna's shoulder and let the sadness wash over him. It was over and the town was safe. But, he just wished he could tell Agatha face to face.

The next few days were a blur of activity. People worked together to clean up the debris and repair broken windows, doors, and other items damaged by the storm. The people of the town and all across the world reached out to Caleb and shared their relief that the danger had passed. While he monitored his social media accounts, Caleb stayed in touch with the first responders. He heard that the police department planned to send an officer out to the sinkholes to pull the caution tape and assess the area. They said they would call for additional clean-up if it seemed necessary.

The officer that arrived on the scene pulled the tape and looked around. He saw blue skies, nothing purple, and looked up at the sky to feel the warm sun on his face. Strangely, he suddenly felt a chill that made his shoulders shake and caused his breath to hitch. He looked around, scanning the area for something that looked out of place. He saw nothing, and the feeling went away. He decided he was just overtired. He climbed back into his vehicle and drove back to town. He radioed the dispatcher on the way. "This is Officer Johnson. I am leaving the sinkholes. We have an all-clear. I repeat, we have an all-clear at the sinkholes."

As he drove away, several sets of purple eyes watched him depart as they sat in their small pool of purple slime.

ABOUT THE AUTHOR

Kelli Hicks is an educator and writer who lives in Tampa, Florida. She has been a classroom teacher, administrator, trainer, and content developer. She has written more than forty books for children.